Paul David Silverman Is A Father

Paul David Silverman Is A Father

by MOLLY CONE

with photographs by HAROLD ROTH

A SKINNY BOOK

E. P. DUTTON   NEW YORK

Text copyright © 1983 by Molly Cone
Photographs copyright © 1983 by Harold Roth

All rights reserved. No part of this publication may be reproduced or transmitted in any form or by any means, electronic or mechanical, including photocopy, recording, or any information storage and retrieval system now known or to be invented, without permission in writing from the publisher, except by a reviewer who wishes to quote brief passages in connection with a review written for inclusion in a magazine, newspaper, or broadcast.

Library of Congress Cataloging in Publication Data

Cone, Molly.
Paul David Silverman is a father.

(A Skinny book)

Summary: Two teenagers get married when they find that they are expecting a baby, and undergo unforeseen trials and adjustments.
[1. Marriage—Fiction. 2. Pregnancy—Fiction.
3. Babies—Fiction] I. Roth, Harold, ill. II. Title.
PZ7.C7592Pa 1983 [Fic] 82-18205
ISBN 0-525-44050-X

Published in the United States by E. P. Dutton, Inc., 2 Park Avenue, New York, N.Y. 10016

Published simultaneously in Canada by Clarke, Irwin & Company Limited, Toronto and Vancouver

Editor: Ann Durell   Designer: Claire Counihan

Printed in the U.S.A.   First Edition
10 9 8 7 6 5 4 3 2 1

THANKS

Harold Roth, the photographer, gratefully thanks:
Justin Bakal
Sheri Fertig
Joshua Singer
Beverly Sperling
Leon Sperling
who posed for the photographs in this book.

LaGuardia Hospital
where photographs were taken.

Ira Cooper and the firm of Cooper & Cappellani
for the use of their private library.

Robin Roth
a special thanks for her help as an assistant.

1

He sat in the Fathers' Waiting Room, not feeling like a father. Waiting. With a magazine on his lap and his heart in his mouth.

If Cathy could see him, she would laugh, he thought. He could always depend on her to laugh. That's what he liked most about her—her laugh.

Who else would fall in love with a girl because of a laugh? Who else but Paul David Silverman: age sixteen, father dead, mother kosher, no siblings that he knew of.

The best day of his life was the day he first heard Cathy laugh. That was the moment he

had decided she was the girl he was going to marry. But it took a long time to get her to agree. Time—and getting pregnant.

Paul looked at the magazine fallen open on his lap. *Three out of five teenage marriages end in divorce,* he read. He quickly turned the page.

It had been a big joke at first. That's the way he had treated the pregnancy—like a big joke. On themselves.

"Baby?" he had said when the doctor told them she was pregnant. "How do you spell that?"

Cathy had laughed.

But she wasn't laughing when they walked out of the clinic.

She stood at the bus stop and muttered little words under her breath.

"It's not so bad," he said. And suddenly it seemed funny. Cathy—who never forgot to do her homework, never forgot her lunch money, never forgot anything—had forgotten to take the pill.

Paul laughed.

"It's not funny to me," Cathy said.

She pushed away from him, into the bus and

down the aisle. She flopped onto an empty seat.

Paul dropped his fare into the money box and hurried after her.

"Look, Cathy," he said. "It's no big deal. We planned on getting married sometime anyway."

She sat with her purse on her lap and a wooden look on her face. "We didn't plan on having kids. Not while we were still in high school, anyway. What I planned was to go to college. And after that I was planning to go to law school—"

He shrugged. "So first you'll have a baby—"

"I could have an abortion." Her voice was flat.

He said just as flatly, "You're having the baby."

Cathy glared at him Her eyes were the shade of jade.

"Sure," she said. "A baby won't change *your* plans any. We'll have the monster, and it won't bother you much. You won't be the one who has to quit school and forget about a career and—" Her voice was getting soupy.

She turned her head halfway around like an owl and blinked at the telephone poles passing along the street.

"You're out of your mind," he said. "It isn't going to be like that. Our marriage will be a partnership. An equal partnership. We'll even draw up a contract to make it strictly equal." He grinned. "You can put in all the big words seeing as you're the one who's going to be the lawyer."

Her head came around again. The hard color of her eyes was softening to pea-soup green. She sniffled and dug into her pocket to pull out a wad of tissues. With it came a small plastic case. It dropped into her lap. The pill. Ruefully she picked it up. She stuck the pill case back into her pocket.

He said helpfully, "Maybe they'll give us a refund."

Of course she laughed. He had expected her to laugh.

2

Paul heard a squeak of foam soles and looked up quickly.

"Mr. Silverman?"

The magazine slipped to the floor as Paul jumped to his feet.

"You can watch the delivery if you wish," the doctor told him.

"Okay," said Paul.

"We'll let you know when we're ready."

"Okay," he said again and sat down.

He picked up the magazine and set it on the low table before him. Then he picked it up again to turn it right side up. He shifted the other magazines so that they formed a neat stack.

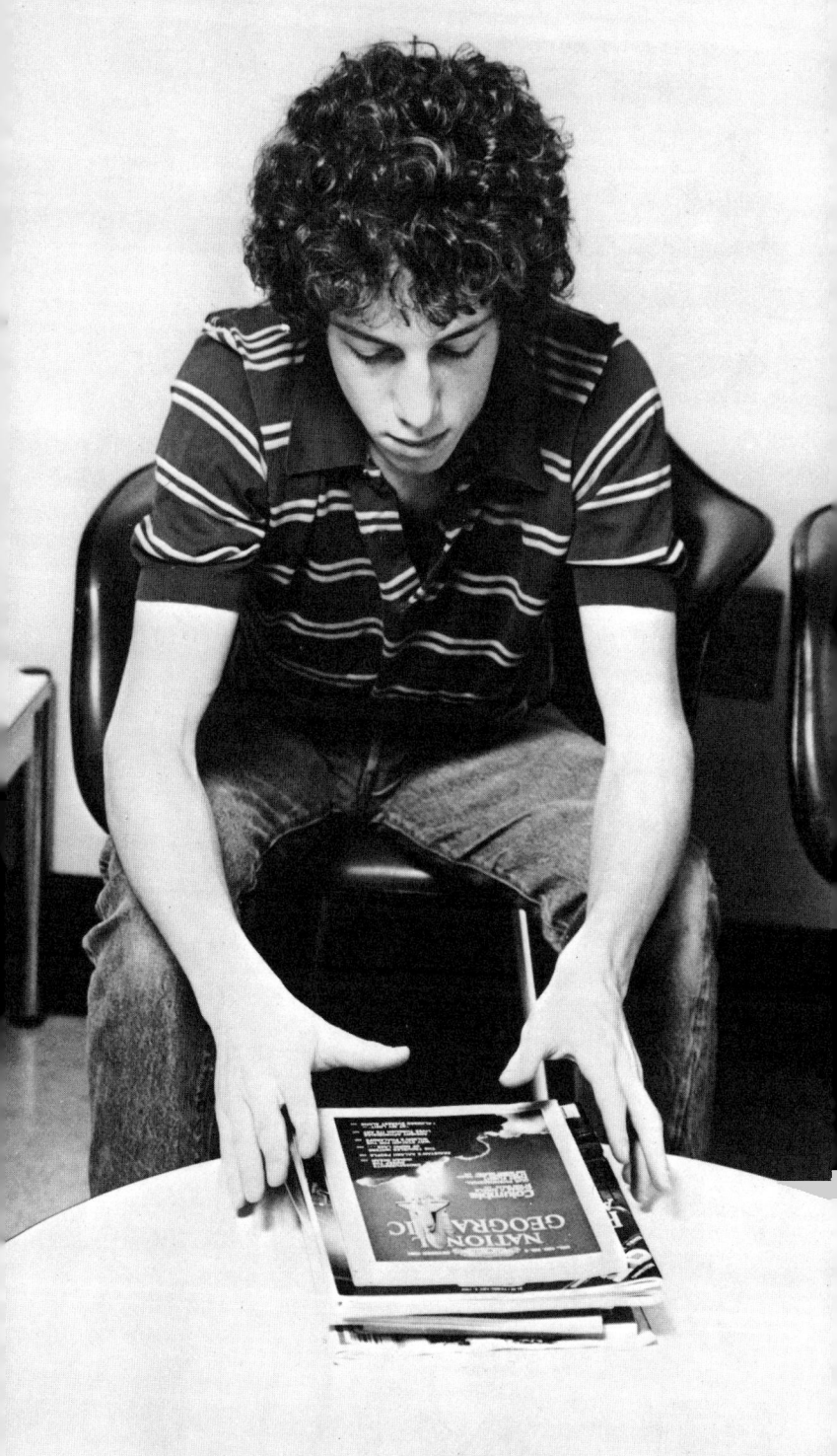

Finally, he emptied the ashtray into the waste can standing in the corner.

He liked things neat. He always had. So did Cathy.

His mother's place was littered with stuff. Chairs sat arm in arm with sofas. Big tables hatched small tables. Ashtrays crowded against cut-glass bowls. His mother's idea of cozy was covering every square inch of space.

Even the old family pictures stood elbow to elbow on the tables and frame to frame on the walls. There was only one that he really liked to look at. It was a wedding photograph.

The groom's face was beardless. His chin was pressed against an old-fashioned stiff collar. His eyes looked out with an unwavering gaze. The girl-bride beside him held her left hand over her chest. On her finger was her gold wedding band.

Paul's Great-great-grandfather Jacob was married at sixteen. That was almost the only thing Paul knew about him. Jacob to Sarah.

"Oh my god!" his mother said when Paul told her that Cathy was pregnant and they were getting married. Her forehead folded itself into some well-worn creases. His mother was a first-class worrier.

She asked him a million questions.

"Where will you live?"

"We'll find a place to rent."

"With what?"

"I'll get a job."

"What about school?"

"I'll go to school too."

"How do you expect to keep up with school and work too?"

"I'll manage."

"And what about Cathy? How is she going to go to school and keep house and cook and—"

"I'm going to help."

"You're a dreamer," she said. "It's not going to work."

"It's going to work," he said stubbornly.

He and his mother butted heads a lot. They never saw eye to eye about anything.

But she gave him a wedding ring to give to Cathy. It was the gold band that had been on the finger of the bride in the picture.

3

Cathy's father hadn't looked at the pregnancy as a gift from heaven either.

He couldn't understand why Cathy wasn't getting married in a church. Paul thought that was funny, because Mr. Martin never went to church.

They didn't bother to tell him that they were writing their own marriage vows. They scratched the words "honor and obey" and "till death do us part." They kept "in sickness and in health," then took it out. They wrote and rewrote until the right words came, and they were both satisfied.

Standing before Judge Markel in Cathy's father's house, they spoke the marriage lines they had written.

> And we shall live together,
> as long as we love each other,
> sharing equally
> the joys and duties
> of marriage.

"Good Lord!" burst out Cathy's father.

Paul heard his mother try to cover with a loud "Amen!"

The kids from school tried not to laugh.

"Did I ever tell you that my Grandfather Jacob was married when he was sixteen?" Paul whispered as he pushed the old gold band onto Cathy's finger.

"I didn't even know that you had a Grandfather Jacob," she muttered back.

"Wait a minute." Paul's mother moved forward. She dug into the embroidered bag hanging from her wrist, and pulled out a small thin wine glass. Quickly she wrapped it in her handkerchief.

"Here," she said and bent to place it on the floor at Paul's feet.

Obediently, Paul raised his foot and stamped

down hard. The crunch of glass breaking brought an approving nod from his mother.

"I now pronounce you Husband and Wife," the judge said firmly.

"It's an old family custom," Paul's mother said loudly to Cathy's father over the shrieking of their children's school friends.

"So is this." Cathy's father poured himself a good splash of gin from the bottle on the table.

He didn't offer it to the wedding guests. They were all under age.

Mrs. Silverman helped herself. *"L'Hyem!"* she said raising her glass to Paul and Cathy. "To life!"

Paul stopped kissing the bride and raised his head.

"L'Hyem to my Grandfather Jacob!" he yelled.

4

Paul looked up. He was still sitting in the hospital waiting room. Waiting.

Across from him sat a man slouched in a plastic-cushioned chair. The ashtray on the table in front of him held a crumpled candy wrapper.

"You were grinning," said the man. "You looked like you were grinning in your sleep."

"I wasn't asleep," said Paul.

The man gave him a considering look. "You waiting for your mother?"

"No," said Paul.

"Oh. Well, I guess this is as good a place to

sit as any. Me, I'm waiting for my wife to have twins."

"Twins?"

"Yup. Danged if my wife isn't having her second set of twins." He loosened his collar and rubbed his neck. "Excuse me," he said, getting up. "I'm going down to the coffee shop and get myself a decaf."

Paul watched him go. He wondered what it would be like to be the father of twins. He couldn't even imagine what it was going to be like as the father of one child, let alone two.

He emptied the ashtray again, set it back on the table, then walked quickly down the hall to the nurses' station. "Is everything all right?" he asked.

The white-capped lady looked at him blankly a moment, then checked something on a chart. The telephone buzzed, and she answered it before she said, "We'll call you when your wife goes into the delivery room."

Paul went back and sat down.

Uneasily he thought about having twins. There was barely enough room in their bedroom for a small-sized crib. They didn't even have the crib yet. Only a basket.

The apartment didn't look like much. But it was cheap.

"There goes the last of my Bar Mitzvah money," Paul had joked as he handed over the first month's rent. The landlady looked at them both suspiciously when Cathy laughed.

They made brick-and-board shelves on one wall of the living room for Paul's records and hung shelves for Cathy's books on the other. There was still plenty of room for the Goodwill dining-room table, which was round, pockmarked, and had claw feet. It was not a thing of beauty, but they liked the crack down the middle which divided it into two halves. He studied on one side. She studied on the other.

Paul kept his bike on his side of the room next to his stereo equipment. Cathy kept hers parked on her side behind the sofa. Even the bed was divided. She liked to sit on her side writing poetry. He lay on his side with earphones on his head and his big toes wiggling to the sound of the Rolling Stones.

He used the bathroom first in the morning. She used it first in the evening. They divided the medicine cabinet evenly—the top two shelves his; the lower two hers. There was one towel bar. Cathy's towel was always on the left side of it. Paul's towel was always on the right.

Neatness was definitely one thing he and Cathy had in common. Both dropped their

Blueprint for a Perfect Marriage

And we shall live together,
as long as we love each other,
sharing equally
the joys and duties
of marriage.

The following is a contract between
the party of the first part
and the party of the second part.

Paul David Silverman	Cathy Martin Silverman
Attend school	Attend school
Cook	Shop
Vacuum	Laundry
Empty trash	Clean bathroom
Dust	Make bed
Keep grocery list	Do dishes

candy wrappers into the wastebasket. Both made lists of everything they planned to do. Both arrived too early rather than too late. And both solemnly agreed to the contract that made their marriage an equal partnership.

They had drawn it up together. When it was finished, it really pleased them both, even though it sounded like a High Holiday Festival litany. Who should cook and who should shop, who should do the dishes and who the laundry, who should vacuum the floor and who should scrub the toilet. Everything was spelled out, split half and half. A blueprint for a perfect marriage.

Cathy had framed it, and Paul hung it over the doorway between the bedroom and living room.

5

"I brought you a noodle pudding," Paul's mother had said on her first visit. She set it down in the kitchenette. She also set down the bag full of groceries she had brought.

"A *noodle* pudding?" Cathy uncovered the dish and peered inside.

"My mother's always liked noodle pudding," Paul explained.

Mrs. Silverman took off her sweater and laid it over the back of a chair. "Everybody raves about my noodle pudding," she said.

"I never did," Paul reminded her, just to keep the record straight.

His mother paid no more attention to his words than she ever had. But it didn't make any difference because his remark made Cathy laugh.

"I brought you a fresh chicken fryer." She burrowed down into the paper bag. "Already cut up. And some short ribs. I brought some catsup too. The spicy kind." She pulled out an extra large bottle. "You always like catsup with short ribs."

Paul put the bottle into the cupboard. He always liked spicy catsup on short ribs because he had never much liked his mother's short ribs.

"I wrote down the recipe for you," his mother said to Cathy. She dug into her purse and pulled out a file card.

"I cook," Paul said taking the card. "Cathy shops."

His mother gazed at him as if he had gone crazy.

"Our marriage is an equal partnership," he explained.

Paul pointed to the contract. "Between the party of the first part and the party of the second part." Everything set forth in legal style. Even Steven. His and hers. They had put all the dirty jobs onto slips of paper and put them in the salad bowl Cathy's friends had given them as a wedding gift. Then they took turns picking. Simple? Not only simple. Brilliant.

"After the baby comes, Cathy will go to school in the morning. I'll go in the afternoon." He snapped his fingers. "Presto! No problems."

His mother picked up her sweater.

"So what's the matter with it?" Paul knew his mother's face. Her face talked. Even before her mouth said anything.

"From your mouth to God's ears," she said. And she reached out to pat Cathy on the cheek. "Your wishes should only come true."

Paul had to laugh.

6

Cathy's father had come to inspect their new home too. He parked in the street and walked up the cracked cement driveway that was tufted with grass and weeds. He hesitated every few steps as if he wasn't sure what he might be stepping on.

Paul stood back while Cathy gave him the tour of their two rooms plus the nook that was the kitchen and the closet made over into a bath.

"Good Lord," he said when he saw the nude on the shower curtain Paul's friends gave them. He backed out and stood in the middle of their living room with his elbows held close to his body as if he was afraid they might touch the walls.

He didn't bring groceries. All he brought was a check. Made out to Cathy, Paul noticed.

The next day, Paul went out and got himself a job. In a recording studio. For after school and some nights. He'd been hanging around recording studios most of his life.

"It was easy," he bragged to Cathy. "After all, who else could they get for next to nothing?"

But he loved the job. It was his kind of job. In one week they promoted him to sound technician helper.

Sometimes he operated the mixer in the studio himself. He listened to the sounds coming from different places like recordings and microphones, and blended or faded or substituted to get a good mix. It was like nothing else.

"I'm a mixer," he announced to Cathy. He strutted around their claw-footed table.

"If you ask me, you're a whole darn Cuisinart," she said.

But he hated to open a joint checking account where he had to let his money mix with her father's checks.

On the other hand, she got really cross at getting things in the mail addressed to Mrs. Paul Silverman. "I feel like I'm opening someone else's mail," she complained.

"Whose?"

"Your mother's, I guess."

"My mother's!"

"Well, her name is Mrs. Silverman, isn't it?"

"So is yours."

"No, it isn't," she said. "I mean I don't feel like a Mrs. Silverman. I still feel like Cathy Martin. Anyway I think it's stupid to have to change my name just because I'm married. It's like having to wear someone else's clothes. And I'm not someone else. I'm me!"

"And then some—" Grinning, Paul fixed his glance on her bulging stomach.

She looked down and made a face.

The baby was nothing either of them looked forward to. Sure, they did all the right things. They read the right books, took the right classes. Paul even swallowed all the right vitamins along with Cathy—just to hear her laugh.

But it wasn't real. Cathy's pregnancy was only a nuisance to be endured. Most of the time, Paul managed to pretend it wasn't even there.

"Monster!" Cathy complained when her stomach was too big for her to sit comfortably. "It's going to be a monster." It was another of their jokes.

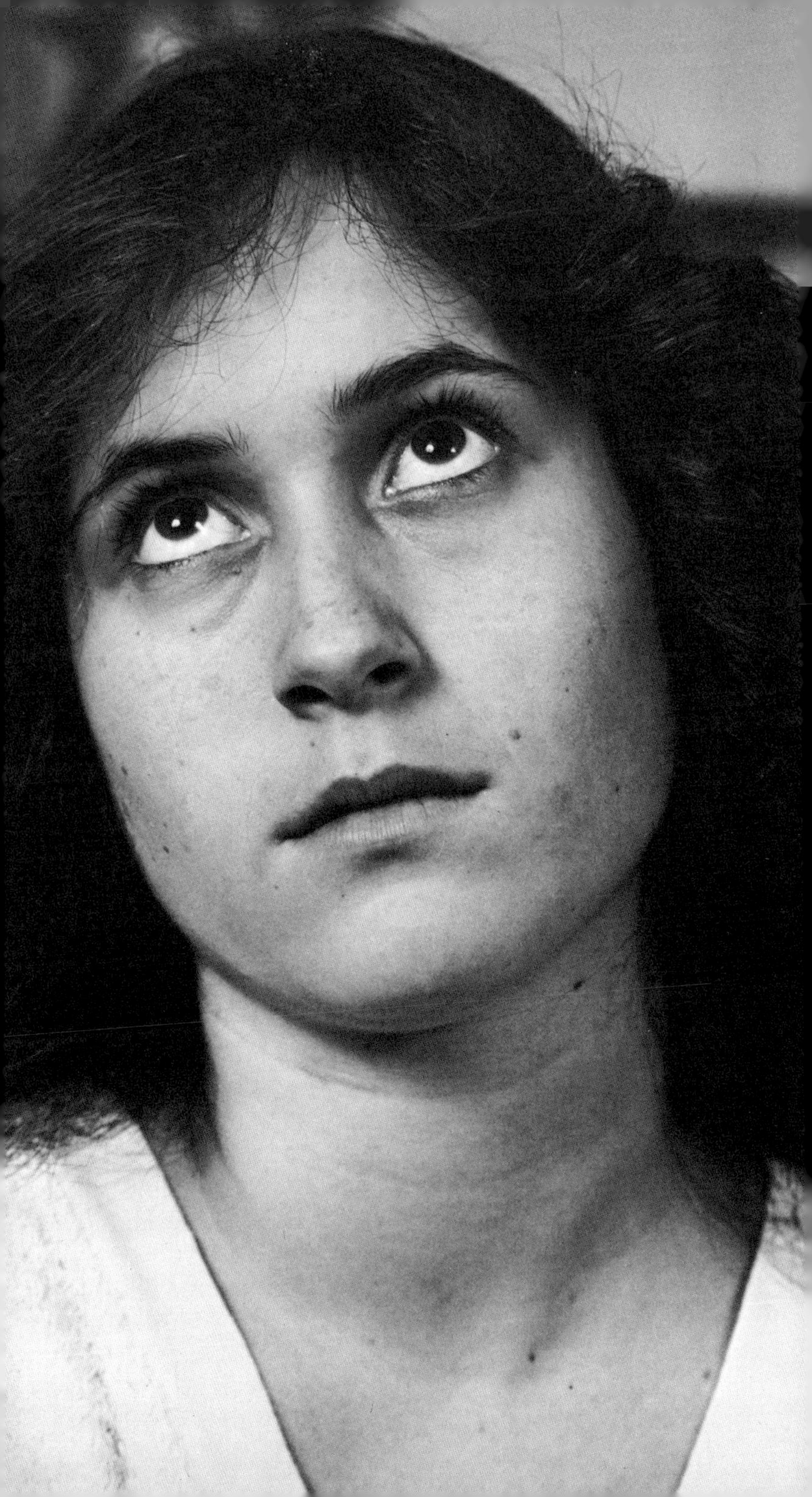

7

Paul heard the squeak of the nurse's shoes as she came toward him. She was pretty when she smiled.

"If you want to watch the delivery, we're about ready now."

He hurried after her and changed fast into the wrinkled green cloth pants and coat and mask the orderly handed him. His heart was beating strangely when he walked into the delivery room.

Cathy was already on a narrow table with her knees high under sheets. They told him to stand behind her and watch through a slanted mirror above. They told him to talk if he wanted to.

Paul tried to say thank you, but only a high squeak came out, as if his voice were still changing.

Cathy put up her hand, the hand with the gold wedding band that had been his Grandmother Sarah's. He held to it tightly and felt his face turn sweaty under the close covering of the surgical mask.

Then—suddenly almost—it was all over. He was standing there hanging on to Cathy's fingers. In the doctor's hands was a screaming red kid with skinny feet, a big wide-open mouth and wet black hair.

"He's not a monster—" Paul couldn't help saying. "He's only a peewee!"

Cathy laughed.

"You're pretty young to be a father, aren't you?" a nurse said when Paul came visiting with a stack of books on baby care borrowed from the library.

Paul started to tell her that his Grandfather Jacob had had three children before he was nineteen. But she had already whizzed the

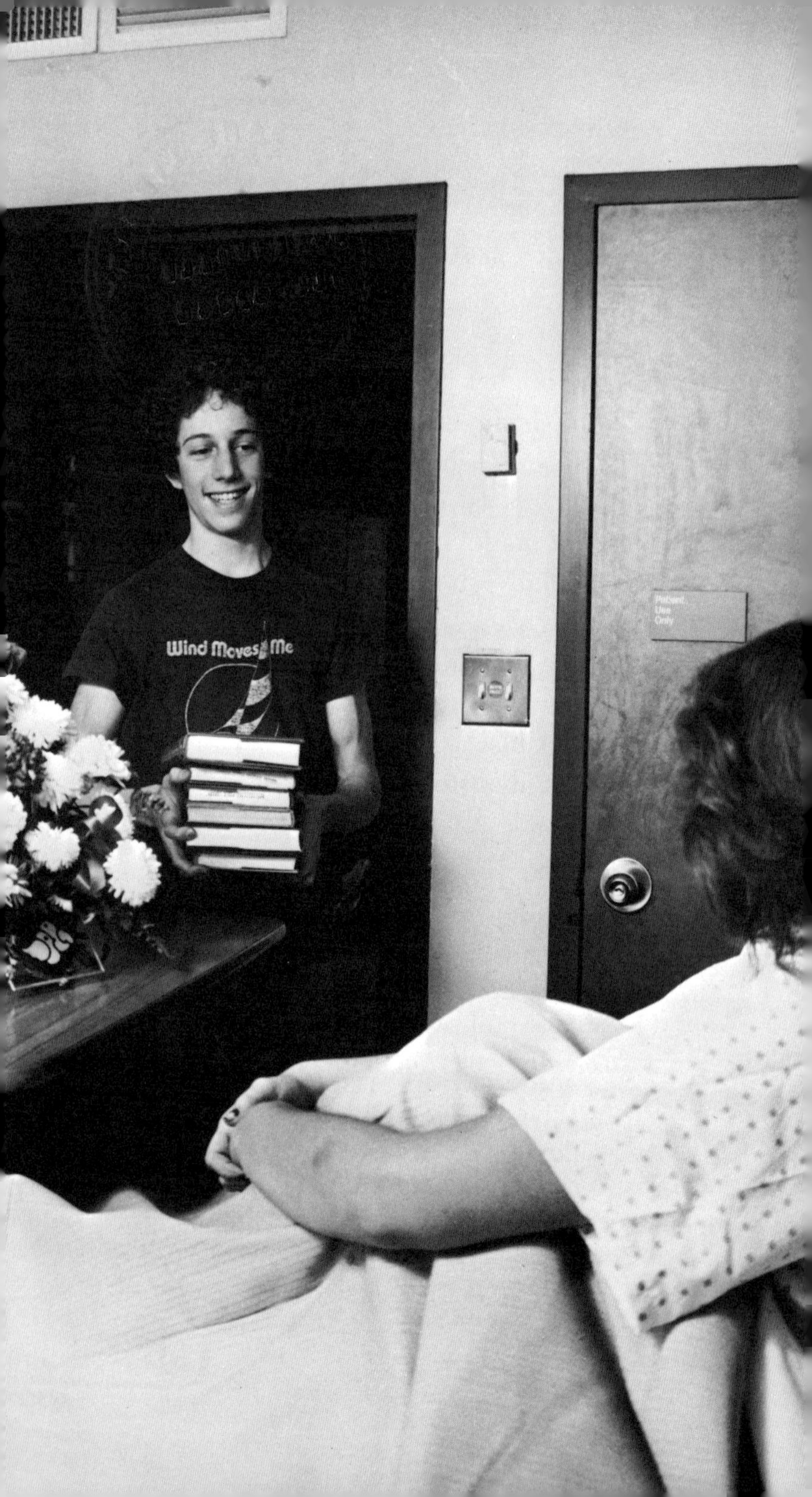
Wind Moves Me

empty lunch dishes onto the cart and was pushing it toward the door.

He told Cathy instead.

"Three babies!" Cathy said, sitting up on her hospital bed with her feet dangling. "How am I ever going to get to law school if we're going to have three babies!"

"I'll stay home while you go to college," said Paul, "and you'll stay home while I—"

"No way," Cathy said.

"We'll all five go to college together?" Paul suggested helpfully.

She threw her bedroom slipper at him.

"I'll hold him," Paul offered in the taxi on the way home.

Cathy pushed his arm away with her shoulder. "That's all right," she said. "I'm holding him."

Paul turned down the corner of the blanket and stared at the wrinkled face under the black hair. The fists were tiny knots.

"Hi, Peewee," he said.

Cathy laughed.

He insisted on carrying Peewee from the car up to the door. A banner screamed PAUL

DAVID SILVERMAN IS A FATHER. Courtesy of his classmates.

"Let me hold him now," said Cathy.

In the middle of the night, Paul thought he heard a sound from the basket in the corner, and he sat up in bed. He listened, heard nothing. Then, to make sure, he threw back his side of the covers and went to see.

Peewee was asleep. Gently Paul lifted the blue coverlet, stuck his hand under the baby's bottom, and felt. Warm. And wet. Carefully he unsnapped the bottom part of the sleeping sack and changed the wet diaper.

He stood there for a long while smiling down at the little guy. Paul didn't mind being a father, he thought suddenly. He didn't mind at all.

"Getting married is the best thing that ever happened to me," Cathy said sleepily when Paul got back into bed again.

"That's what my Grandmother Sarah thought too," he told her.

"How would you know?"

"Because my Grandfather Jacob said so."

She laughed.

8

"He looks just like me," Paul told his mother when she arrived with three bags of groceries and a knitted sweater for Peewee.

He held the kid cradled in his arm, with the warm round head pressing into his armpit. He half turned so his mother could get a good look. "He does, doesn't he?"

"Who knew how you looked?" his mother said. "All you did was scream for three months." She bent her head to cluck at Peewee.

Paul felt a kind of pride when Peewee's eyes opened wide. He seemed to regard his grandmother with a searching stare, then turned his head and yawned.

"He's got your mouth all right," Mrs. Silverman said.

Paul laughed. His mother had a sense of humor. Funny that he had never realized it before.

"He's got the Silverman nose too," Paul pointed out.

"Don't worry about it," his mother said. "Maybe he'll look more like Cathy's family later."

"Not a chance," Paul said loudly. "This is my kid."

Cathy's father came too. With another check. "I think he's suffering from dollaritis," Paul cracked after Mr. Martin left, but Cathy was already jumping up to take another look at Peewee.

She was always jumping up, it seemed to Paul during the next few weeks, to look at Peewee, even when Paul had just been in to check on him.

"How are things going?" His mother called every day to ask that question.

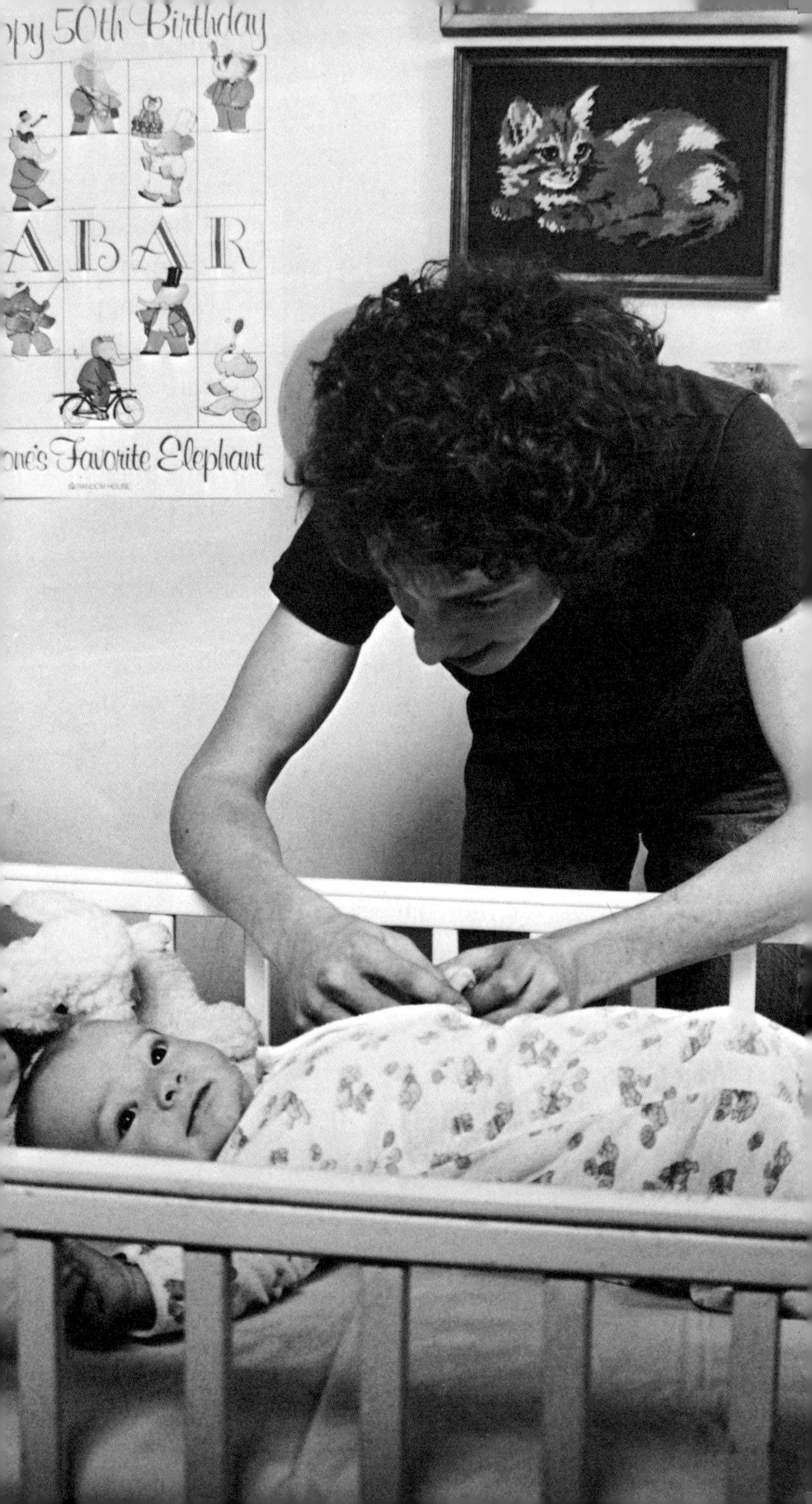
ppy 50th Birthday
ABAR
one's Favorite Elephant

"He's asleep," Paul would say, because that seemed to be what she always wanted to hear.

Paul discovered that his mother thought a baby wasn't a good baby unless he was asleep. He guessed that's where his mother had started misunderstanding him. He had never needed much sleep.

A crib in the corner had replaced the basket. But Peewee never wanted to waste much time sleeping either. He lay awake gurgling when Paul turned up the Rolling Stones on his stereo system. Peewee loved the Rolling Stones. No "Rock-a-bye Baby" for him.

He also loved floating on his back in the bathtub with Paul's hand stretched under his bottom for support. And having his stomach splashed, and chasing the floating soap. And eating. Peewee was a good eater.

That was another one of his mother's favorite phrases, Paul reflected. After you passed the good baby test, the next one was to be a good eater.

Since she had once told him that he had always spit up half of everything that went down, Paul figured he had flunked that one too. But Peewee didn't. He never spit up anything—very much.

"You're not giving him French fries," Cathy screeched when she came home early one day while he and Peewee were still eating lunch. That is, Paul was eating lunch. Peewee was mostly kibitzing.

"It's okay," he told her calmly. "He likes French fries."

"Nobody feeds a baby French fries!" she insisted.

"He won't tell anybody." Paul grinned at her, but she didn't laugh.

"I'm skipping school today, and Peewee and I are going to go look at turntables down at Radio Shack," he told her, plucking a potato bit from his son's chin and swabbing at his face with a paper napkin.

She stood there looking at him a moment, her eyes glinting. But when Peewee gurgled at her, they turned soft as pea soup.

"No you're not," said Cathy. "Peewee is mine in the afternoon. Remember?"

She took Peewee out of his high chair then, removed his bib and carried him with her into the bedroom.

"All right for you. I'll go all by myself!" he hollered in at her.

She didn't laugh then either.

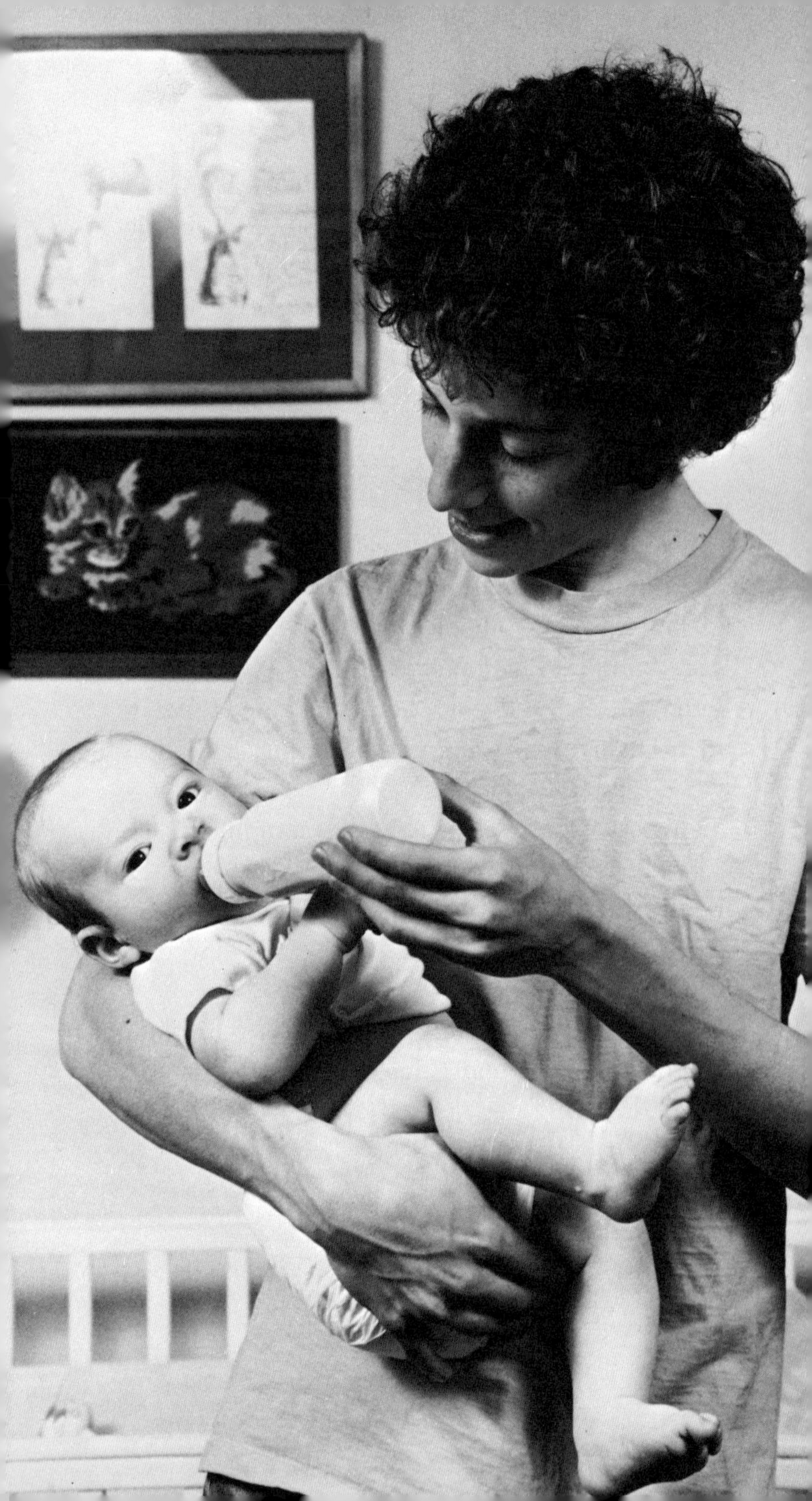

The next morning, with Peewee comfortable in the crook of his arm, guzzling his milk, it occurred to Paul that he hadn't heard Cathy laugh at him the way she used to for a long time.

He thought about that as he gazed down at the swirl of hair on top of Peewee's head and tipped up the bottle. When the milk was all gone, he gently pulled the nipple out of the still-sucking mouth. It sounded like a stopper coming out of a bathtub.

Carefully, he hoisted the sleepy kid to his shoulder and patted gently until he was rewarded with a loud burp. Loud enough to start the horses down the track. He had to laugh.

9

When Paul got home that night after work, there was a note under the magnet on the refrigerator door. "You did NOT empty the garbage," it said.

He pulled open the door under the sink. The sack was overflowing. It was also leaking, and when he picked it up, it split.

He got into bed a little later and turned on the lamp. Cathy groaned.

"Why did you let the garbage pail get so putrid?" he yelled at her.

She flopped over to her other side. "Not my job," she mumbled and fell asleep again.

Paul lay there with his hands behind his

head and his eyes wide open. He tried to figure out what was going wrong. What was it that had made marriage go "right" for his Grandfather Jacob?

Paul tried to picture the wedding photograph hanging in his mother's house. She had once told him that Grandfather Jacob and his bride had not even known each other before the day they were married. It had been an arranged marriage. The first time they were alone was on their wedding night.

Paul found himself staring at the pile of laundry on the chair on his side of the room. He hadn't bothered to fold anything. Cathy's job.

He closed his eyes. But he couldn't go to sleep. He sat up and slid out of bed. Peewee slept with his face down and his bottom up in the air. He looked like a cabbage growing. His black hair had turned brown. It was beginning to curl, Paul noticed—exactly like his.

Paul turned him over and changed him.

He looked at the stack of baby clothes lying on the dresser. Cathy had folded them. Paul shook out each little garment, smoothed it flat on top of the dresser and folded it again. He put them in the top drawer.

Then he wiped off the top of the changing

table with a tissue. He put the paper diaper into the covered pail, and took the other damp things into the bathroom. He stuck them into the hamper and turned on the faucet to wash his hands.

There was nothing in the dish on the basin. He looked around. No soap. "Damn," he muttered and used some of the liquid in the baby-shampoo bottle instead.

"We're all out of soap," he told Cathy when he got back into bed.

"Well if you had put it on the list, I would have purchased it," she said and yawned.

He said, "I put tomato sauce on the list last week, and you didn't purchase that."

She threw back the covers and flung herself out of bed. He followed her into the other room.

"Why do you have to act like you're the only one who does anything right?" she shouted.

"Why do you always have to act like everything I do is wrong?" he yelled.

She laughed then. Not the laugh he loved. It was a hoot.

"You know what?" she said. "It was dumb of us to get married. Plain dumb. We didn't really know each other well enough."

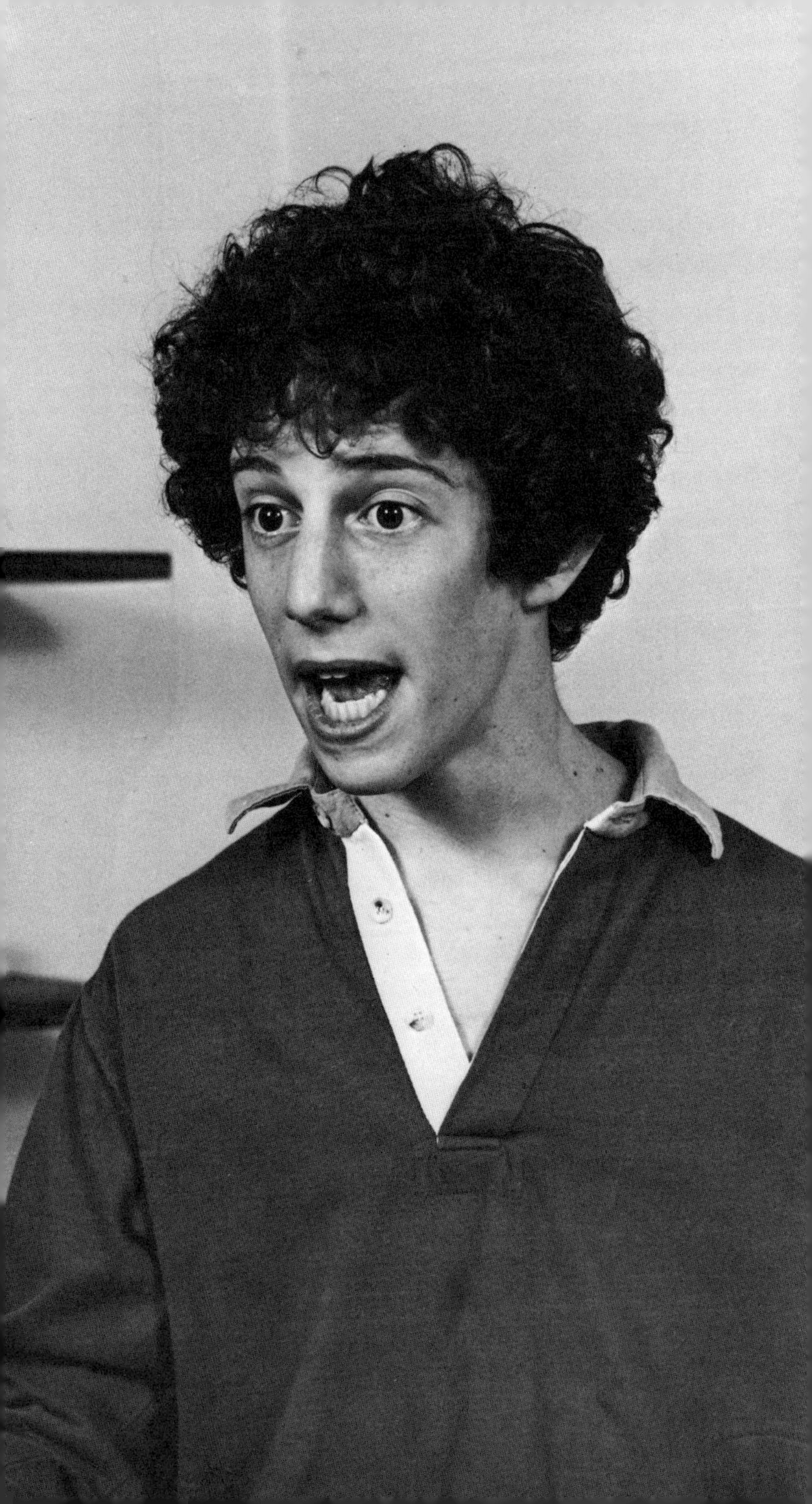

He started to tell her that his Grandfather Jacob and his Grandmother Sarah didn't know each other either—

"And don't tell me about your Grandfather Jacob!" she warned. "Don't you dare tell me one more thing about your Grandfather Jacob!"

Paul shut his mouth, turned and went back into the bedroom. He slammed the door. Peewee woke up. Paul got to him first.

He picked up his son, warmed his bottle, fed him, and got him back into his crib again. When he looked into the living room, Cathy was sitting on the sofa. She had a sweater over her shoulders, and was staring at a magazine.

"Come on back to bed," he said.

She didn't answer. She turned the page.

"All right!" he shouted. "So you go to bed, and I'll sleep on the sofa!"

10

She was gone when he awoke the next morning.

And so was Peewee.

Paul stared at the empty crib for a moment. He pulled open the top dresser drawer. Empty too.

He dashed into the kitchen. There was no baby bottle on the drainboard. He opened the refrigerator. No baby food on the shelves.

"DAMN!" he shrieked.

He called her father's house. No one answered.

He pulled a scrap of paper out from under

the claws of the table. But it wasn't a note. It was just one of Cathy's poems. A three-line poem she called a haiku. He was just about to drop it when his eye caught the first line. And he laid it on the table, and stood leaning on one flat-out hand and read it again.

> Having a baby
> Was incomprehensible
> Until he was born.

He looked at the seventeen syllables a long time.

It was the space over the door that made him look up. It caught his eye because the framed contract wasn't where it was supposed to be. It was on the floor—pulled out of its frame and torn in two.

He picked up the two pieces and fit them back together. The blueprint for a perfect marriage. He stood there reading it all through and almost laughed.

They had drawn a line down the middle of their marriage—like two kids dividing everything into YOURS and MINE. Only they couldn't divide up Peewee.

He let the pieces of the contract fall to the floor again. She was right. It was worthless. An

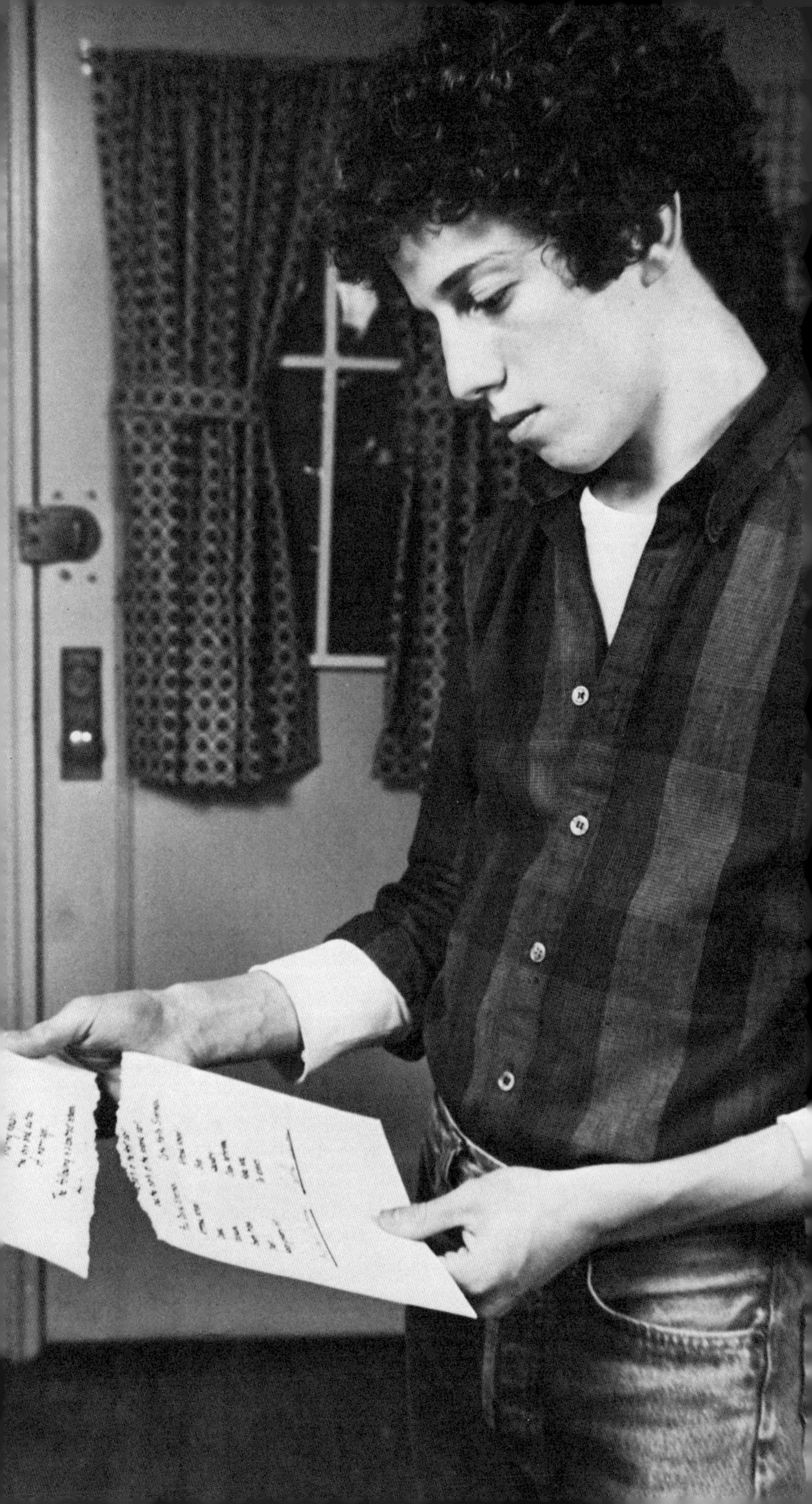

equal partnership in marriage wasn't a matter of simple division.

THREE OUT OF FIVE TEENAGE MARRIAGES END IN DIVORCE. He remembered that suddenly, and his stomach lurched. He and Cathy were already part of those statistics.

The telephone rang, and he jumped to answer it.

"Paul?" It was only his mother.

He couldn't keep from crying—like he was still a kid, instead of a man with a kid of his own.

"Cathy left Peewee here with me for a little while," his mother said. "She just picked him up. I think they were going to the public library."

Paul pulled in a quivering breath.

"I just thought you'd want to know."

"Thanks, Mom," he said. "Thanks a lot."

He found them in the reference section. Cathy's elbows were on the table. Her feet were twined around the legs of the chair. Peewee was asleep in the baby carrier on the table near her.

He sat down next to her. The chair scraped

as he moved it. Her head snapped up. Her face was blotchy, as if she was just starting her period—or maybe she had been crying.

He felt his heart squeezing tight. A marriage was more than an equal partnership.

"Your mother showed me the picture of your Grandfather Jacob." Cathy's fingers were gripping the cover of her book. His grandmother's gold wedding band seemed very thin and very fragile. "You look like him—a little."

"I do?" His voice squeaked.

"Your mother says you're his spitting image—" She was studying her fingers, and there was no expression on her face. "Of course I don't think she meant it as a compliment. . . ."

A hoarse sound erupted from Paul's throat—a laugh. Or half a laugh. He didn't know why, but he suddenly felt not only surprised but pleased. Really pleased.

"She said when your Grandfather Jacob had his mind set on something, the world could turn upside down and he wouldn't notice it."

That sounded exactly like his mother, Paul thought. He cleared his throat. "All I could think of was that you'd walked out on me and taken my kid."

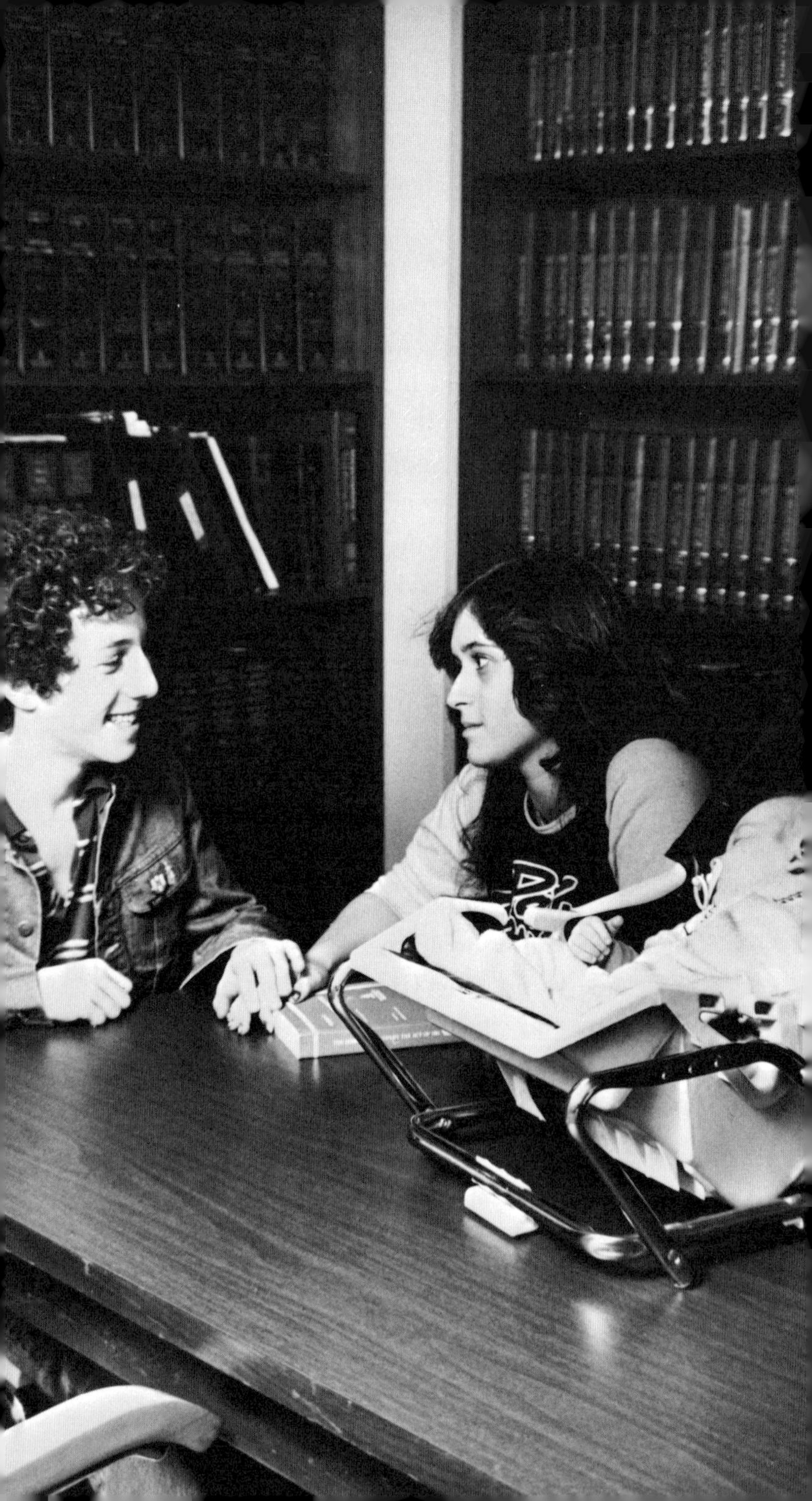

He saw her chin go up. "He's not all yours."

Paul stared down at the sleeping kid. He saw the Silverman blunt nose. Peewee stretched his neck, opened his eyes and closed them again. He had Cathy's eyes and Cathy's chin. Funny, Paul thought, he hadn't noticed the likeness before.

He guessed there were a lot of things about being married he hadn't noticed before. And he began to feel a stir of excitement, as if he were operating the mixer at the studio. Sometimes he had to work at the blending of sounds a long while to get a good mix.

"He's not yours," said Paul. "And he's not mine—he's ours." The word pinged in his head. A clear bright sound.

He couldn't help grinning at Cathy. They weren't kids anymore; they were a family. Two out of every five teenage marriages don't end in divorce.

Cathy smiled. The crinkling at the corners of her mouth would probably be deep lines some day like his mother's.

Which was okay. Because the smile was wonderful.

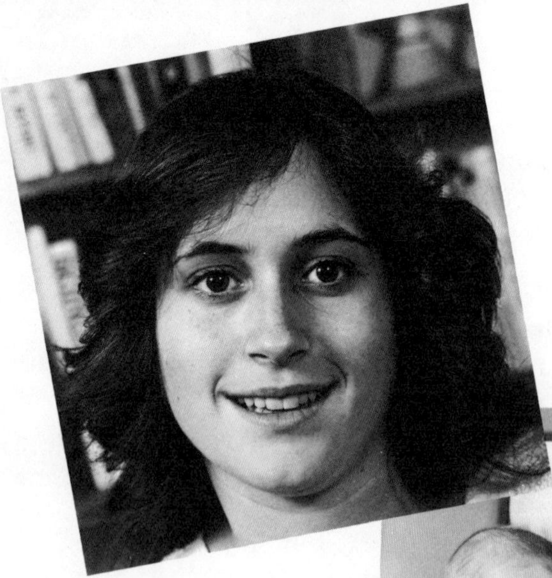

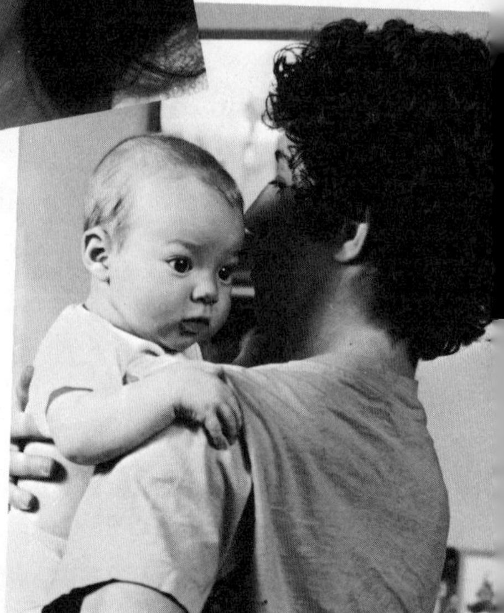

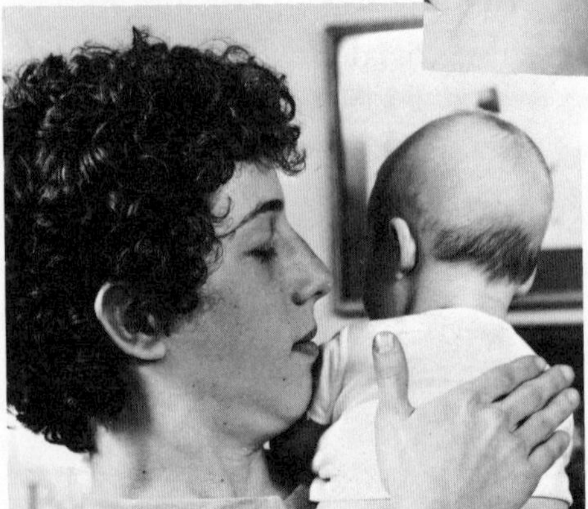

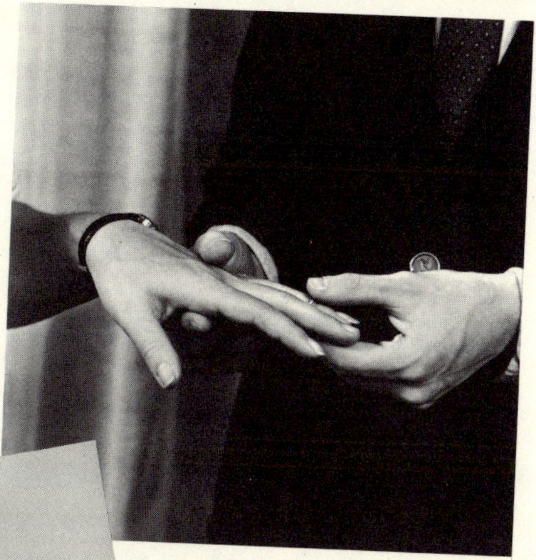

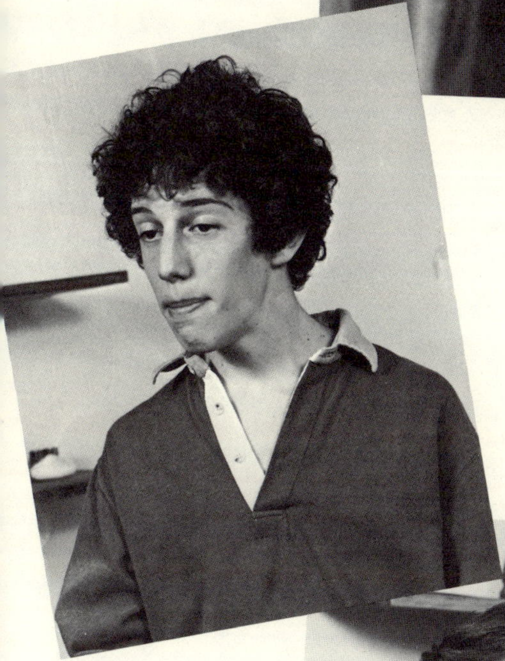

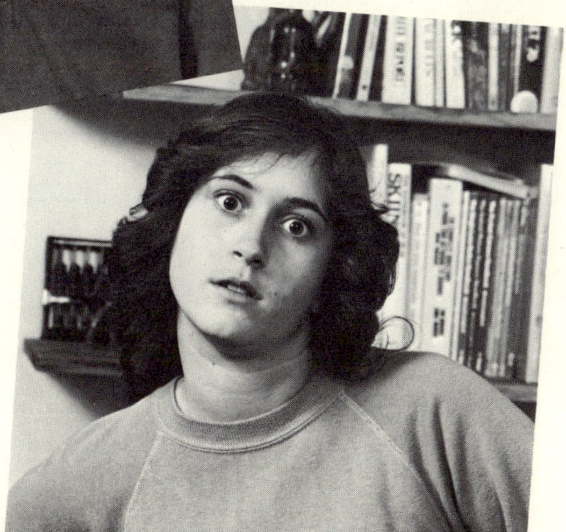